My Secret Unicorn

Dreams Come True

Other books in the series

THE MAGIC SPELL

My Secret Unicorn

Dreams Come True

Linda Chapman

Illustrated by Biz Hull

Cover Illustration by Andrew Farley

AN
APPLE
PAPERBACK

SCHOLASTIC INC.

New York Toronto London Auckland Sydney
Mexico City New Delhi Hong Kong Buenos Aires

ISBN 0-439-60010-3

Text copyright © 2002 by Working Partners Limited
Illustrations copyright © 2002 by Biz Hull
Created by Working Partners Ltd.
All rights reserved. Published by Scholastic Inc.,
557 Broadway, New York, NY 10012, by arrangement with Working Partners Limited.
MY SECRET UNICORN is a trademark of Working Partners Limited.
SCHOLASTIC, APPLE PAPERBACKS, and associated logos are trademarks and/or
registered trademarks of Scholastic Inc.

24 23 22 21 20 19 18 17 16 15 14 13   7   8   9/0

Printed in the U.S.A.   40
First Scholastic printing, January 2004

*To Iola—dreams really
can come true*

My Secret Unicorn

Dreams Come True

CHAPTER

One

"It's almost time, Twilight," Lauren Foster whispered to the gray pony beside her. She looked down at the star-shaped flower in her hand. At the tip of each purple petal, a golden spot glowed. The pony stamped one of his front hooves and pushed at her hand impatiently.

"Just a few more minutes," Lauren told

him. She looked up. The sun had almost set. This was the moment she'd been waiting for all day. As the last of the sun disappeared behind the mountains, a bright star shone overhead.

A thrill ran through Lauren. *Now!*

Gently, she began to crumple the petals of the flower between her fingers. As she did so, she whispered the secret words of the Turning Spell.

Twilight Star, Twilight Star,
Twinkling high above so far.
Shining light, shining bright,
Will you grant my wish tonight?
Let my little horse forlorn
Be at last a unicorn!

Almost before the last word had left Lauren's mouth, there was a bright purple flash.

The patch of grass where Twilight had been standing was empty. Lauren looked up. A snow-white unicorn was cantering in circles in the sky.

"Twilight!" Lauren exclaimed in delight.

With a kick of his back legs, Twilight swooped down and landed beside Lauren.

"Hello," he said, putting his nose close to hers and blowing out softly. Although Twilight's words rang out clearly in Lauren's head, his mouth didn't move. Lauren remembered what he had told her when she had first turned him into a unicorn the night before — as long as she was touching him or holding a hair from his mane, she would be able to hear him speak.

Lauren hugged him and then looked down at the petals still clutched in her hand. "But I didn't throw them on the ground," she said.

Twilight tossed his flowing silver mane. "You don't need to anymore. The moonflower petals are only needed the *first* time the spell is said. You don't even need the light of the Twilight Star. From now on, all you need to do is say the magic words." He pawed the grass. "Come on, Lauren. Let's go flying!"

Lauren didn't need to be asked twice. In a flash, she had scrambled onto his back.

Twilight plunged upward, and Lauren laughed in delight as the wind whipped through her hair. She held on to Twilight's long mane.

"I'm getting better at flying," Twilight said, cantering in a smooth circle.

"Definitely!" Lauren agreed.

The day before, Twilight's flying had been very wobbly, and Lauren had been very glad that special unicorn magic had prevented her from falling off! Now she looked down at the fields and woods below.

"Let's fly over the woods," Twilight
said. "And jump over the treetops."

"OK," Lauren agreed. "But I can't stay

out too long in case Mom and Dad start wondering where I am."

Twilight turned in the air and headed for the forest that covered the mountains behind Lauren's house.

Lauren could see the nearby farms spread out beneath them. One in particular caught her attention — a white clapboard farmhouse with red barns that hugged the mountainside at the edge of the forest. "That's Goose Creek Farm," she said. "Dad met the man who owns it today. His name is Mr. Cassidy. He's got a daughter named Mel who's the same age as me and she's got a pony. Dad arranged for me to go and visit them tomorrow and you're coming, too!"

"Sounds like fun!" Twilight said.

Lauren suddenly looked anxious. "What if Mel's pony guesses you're a unicorn?" she said. She knew that it was very important that no one discover Twilight's secret. Lauren had been given the spell to turn Twilight into a unicorn by an elderly lady named Mrs. Fontana, and she had told Lauren that she must never let anyone find out Twilight was a unicorn. It might put him in great danger!

"He'll know," Twilight said, "but it'll be OK. Horses and ponies understand that a unicorn's secret must be kept."

"Do all animals know about unicorns?" Lauren asked curiously.

Twilight shook his head. "Just horses and ponies, though sometimes other animals will sense I'm different." He swooped down so that his hooves were skimming the treetops. "Now, are you ready to do some jumping?"

"You bet!" Lauren exclaimed.

"Then here goes!" Twilight galloped forward through the air and carried her over the top branches of a tall pine tree.

They leaped from one treetop to the next, giddy with excitement. At the far edge of the forest, Twilight cantered into the air and turned a loop-de-loop. Lauren whooped out loud in delight.

All too soon, Lauren realized it was time to go back home. "If we're gone much longer, Mom and Dad might start to get worried," she said to Twilight.

He nodded, and they flew back to Granger's Farm.

Twilight landed in his paddock. Lauren dismounted and said the Undoing Spell. There was a bright purple flash as Twilight turned from a unicorn into a small gray pony.

"See you tomorrow," Lauren whispered. She gave him a quick hug, then raced back to the house.

Her dad was in the kitchen. He glanced at the kitchen clock. "You've been out a long time," he commented.

"I was just playing with Twilight," Lauren said, her heart pounding.

To her relief, her dad smiled. "I'm glad you're enjoying having a pony so much," he said. "Life here in the country sure beats life back in the city, doesn't it?"

"Totally," Lauren agreed happily. It was only a week ago that her family had left their house in the city to move to Granger's Farm so that Mr. Foster could follow his dream of becoming a farmer. But already Lauren felt completely at home.

As Lauren passed her brother's bedroom, she heard laughter. She pushed the door open. Her brother, Max, was in bed, and Buddy, Max's Bernese mountain dog puppy, was standing on his hind legs with his big white front paws on the covers. His pink tongue was hanging out and he seemed to be trying to lick every inch of Max's face.

"Honestly, Max, I think he'd get into bed with you if I let him!" Mrs. Foster exclaimed as she pushed the black-and-tan puppy down. "Buddy, you're a pest," she scolded, but she smiled as she spoke.

Buddy came gamboling over to Lauren. Not managing to stop in time, he skidded into her legs.

"Oof!" Lauren exclaimed. "Buddy! You weigh a ton!"

"Wait till he's fully grown," Mrs. Foster said with a laugh. "Now, you'd better get ready for bed, too, honey. You and Dad are expected at the Cassidys' house at nine-thirty, so you're going to have to be up early to get Twilight fed and groomed in time."

Lauren nodded.

"I hope you and Mel Cassidy get along," Mrs. Foster went on. "It would be great for you to have a friend to go riding with."

"Yeah," Lauren agreed. "I hope Mel's nice."

As she went to her bedroom, she thought about the next day. Would Mel want to be friends with her? Would she want to be friends with Mel? She hoped so.

She got her pajamas out from under her pillow and walked to her bedroom window. She could see the Blue Ridge Mountains towering up behind the house and, best of all, she could see Twilight's stable and paddock.

"Good night, Twilight," she whispered, looking at the little pony's shadowy shape grazing by the gate. "I hope tomorrow's going to be OK."

Twilight looked up. Lauren was sure she heard him whicker. Blowing him a kiss, she smiled and closed the curtain.

CHAPTER

Two

"Buddy! Here, boy!" Max called, crawling under the kitchen table as Lauren ate her cereal the next morning.

Mr. Foster was standing by the door talking to Hank and Joe, the two farmhands who helped look after the Fosters' herd of dairy cows and the ten pigs. "I want to move the calves to the bottom pasture this morning," Mr. Foster was explaining.

Mrs. Foster was on the phone. "Yes, we're finally getting unpacked," she said, one hand pressed to her ear to shut out the noise in the kitchen.

Lauren got up and put her empty cereal bowl in the dishwasher. "I'm going to get Twilight ready," she announced.

The April sun was shining as she stepped outside, and the new leaves on the trees looked green and fresh. Lauren breathed in deeply and ran down the path that led from the house to the paddock. Twilight was waiting at the gate. He whinnied when he saw her.

"Hi, fella," Lauren said, climbing over the gate. "I bet you'd like some breakfast." Twilight nuzzled her. Snapping the lead rope onto his halter, Lauren led him up to his stable and gave him some pony nuts in a bucket. As he ate, she looked at her watch. 8:15. That meant she had an hour to groom him before she and her dad had to leave for the Cassidys' house.

Half an hour later, Lauren stepped back to admire her handiwork. Twilight's scruffy gray coat was looking much cleaner, his hooves gleamed from the hoof oil, and his newly washed tail was almost dry.

"You look lots better," Lauren declared. He whickered in agreement.

"Buddy! Come back!"

Hearing her brother's cry, Lauren looked around. Buddy was galloping down the path toward her, his black ears flopping, his enormous white paws thudding on the grass. Max tore after him.

"Buddy! Careful!" Lauren gasped as the puppy headed straight for the bucket of water. Buddy tried to stop but he was too late. He crashed into it, sending the dirty suds flying up into the air.

Twilight snorted and jumped back to the end of his rope, but the contents of the bucket splashed all over him.

"Buddy!" Lauren exclaimed. She swung around to Max. He was standing on the path, his hand fixed to his mouth, his blue eyes wide with shock. "Max!" she cried.

"I'm sorry, I'm really sorry," Max said. "I opened the back door, and Buddy just ran off down the path. I couldn't stop him, Lauren."

Lauren sighed. It was no use getting

annoyed with Max. It wasn't his fault that
Buddy was so clumsy. "It's OK," she said.
"I guess I'll just have to groom Twilight
again."

"I'll help you," Max offered.

Lauren took a towel from the grooming
box and handed it to Max. "Thanks," she
said.

"Look at Buddy," Max said suddenly.

Lauren looked at the puppy. He was
crawling on his tummy toward Twilight,
his ears pricked up, his tail wagging like
crazy. "*Woof!*" he said, jumping back.
"*Woof! Woof!*" He sat up and cocked his
head to one side.

"What's he doing?" Max said in
surprise.

"I don't know," Lauren said with a frown. She tried to move the puppy away, but Buddy just kept staring at Twilight. He seemed fascinated. Lauren felt worried. Could Buddy somehow sense that Twilight wasn't a normal pony? She grabbed hold of Buddy's collar again. "Here, Max. Maybe you should take him back to the house. Twilight might step on him by mistake if he gets too close!"

"But what about helping you?" Max said, looking disappointed.

"I'll manage," Lauren replied quickly. She saw Max's mouth open as if to argue. "We don't want Buddy to get hurt, do we?"

"No," Max said, taking Buddy's collar.

As he dragged Buddy back to the house, Lauren bit her lip. If Buddy acted like that in front of her mom and dad, they were bound to get suspicious. She looked at Twilight. He was staring after Buddy, and Lauren was sure he looked concerned.

At 9:15, Lauren rode out of Granger's Farm with her father walking beside Twilight. They headed for Goose Creek Farm. It wasn't far, and they were soon walking down the driveway toward the house. The back door opened and a tall man with black hair came out onto the veranda.

"Mike!" he said, coming forward to greet Mr. Foster. "Hi. And this must be

Lauren. Mel can't wait to meet you. She's
with Shadow at the moment — that's her
pony. Come on, I'll show you to the
paddock."

Lauren rode after him. As they reached
the back of the house, she saw a paddock
with two jumps set out. A dapple-gray
pony was tethered to the paddock fence.
A girl with black curly hair was standing
beside him, brushing his shiny coat.

"Mel!" Mr. Cassidy called.

The girl turned. Seeing Lauren, her
face lit up with a friendly grin. "Hi!" she
called. Throwing her grooming brush
down, she jogged over. "I'm Mel."

"I'm Lauren," Lauren said rather shyly.

"Your pony's gorgeous," Mel said. "What's his name?"

"Twilight," said Lauren, dismounting.

"Twilight." Mel frowned thoughtfully, patting him. "Did he used to belong to Jade Roberts?"

"That's right." Lauren said in surprise.

Mel nodded. "I thought I recognized him. I go to the Pony Club with Jade." She smiled at Lauren. "My pony's name is Shadow. Do you want to come meet him?"

Lauren nodded eagerly.

"We'll leave you two girls to get to know each other, then," Mr. Cassidy said. "We'll be in the house if you want us."

Lauren and Mel nodded. "So, how long have you had Shadow?" Lauren asked as she led Twilight over to say hello.

"Six months," Mel replied. "I couldn't believe it when Mom and Dad bought him for me. I'd wanted a pony for . . . like forever. I think I was born pony-crazy."

"Me, too!" Lauren agreed, grinning at her.

Shadow turned his head to look at Twilight. Lauren held her breath. What if he acted as strangely as Buddy had?

But, after staring at Twilight for a moment, Shadow simply snorted softly and stretched out his muzzle to say hello.

Twilight blew down his nostrils in reply.

"They like each other!" Mel said. She beamed at Lauren. "It's going to be so cool being neighbors — I can just tell!" Happiness welled up inside Lauren.

"I'll get Shadow tacked up," Mel said. "Then we can play catch in the paddock."

Lauren and Mel had a lot of fun. Shadow was fast and could turn very quickly, but Twilight was also pretty fast. They chased each other around the paddock, trying to tag each other, and then they had an egg-and-spoon race, a trotting race, and a race where they had to canter around poles stuck in the ground in a line. "This is a lot better than riding on my own!" Mel said as they finished in a dead heat.

"Shall we jump next?" Lauren asked, looking at the fences.

Mel's face fell. "There's no point." She

sighed. "Shadow doesn't jump. I took him to a Pony Club mounted meeting last month but he wouldn't even go near a jump. Watch."

She cantered Shadow away from Twilight and turned him toward one of the fences. He slowed to a trot and then to a walk. Mel kicked his sides but it made no difference. He stopped a yard away from the jump.

"He does it every time," Mel said, riding back to Lauren. "And I don't know what I'm going to do. There's another mounted meeting this Saturday, and Jade Roberts and her friend Monica were really mean about him when he wouldn't jump last time."

"Maybe he'll follow Twilight over a jump," Lauren suggested.

But even when Twilight jumped, Shadow refused to follow. As soon as Mel turned him toward the fences, he slowed down, his ears back.

"It's no use." Mel sighed. "He's not going to do it." She patted Shadow. "It doesn't matter, Shadow," she said. "I love you whether you can jump or not."

Although Mel tried to smile, Lauren could see the sadness in her new friend's eyes. "I'll try to think of some other way to help," Lauren promised. "If I come over tomorrow after school, maybe we could try again then."

"That would be great," Mel said, looking

more cheerful. "Between the two of us we must be able to think of something."

They untacked the ponies and turned them out into the paddock to graze. Then Mel showed Lauren around Goose Creek Farm. Just up the path from the barn with Shadow's stall was an enormous red hay barn. In it was Mel's cat, Sparkle. "She just had two kittens," Mel said to Lauren. "They're only three weeks old."

Lauren gasped in delight as she saw the two tiny black kittens snuggled into their mother's side. Sparkle had made a nest in a pile of loose hay at the back of the barn, and the two kittens were sleeping beside her.

"What have you named them?" Lauren asked in a low voice.

"Star and Midnight," Mel whispered back. "Mom and Dad said I can keep them both."

As they walked back down the path toward the paddock and the farmhouse, Mel turned to Lauren. "You know, you should join the Pony Club, too. We have mounted and unmounted meetings every month, competitions, and there's even a camp in the summer!"

Lauren hesitated, thinking about the two girls who had been mean to Mel.

Mel seemed to read her mind. "It's only Jade and Monica who are like that," she said. "The others in my group are really nice."

"OK, then," Lauren agreed. "I'll ask."

"You two look like you've been having fun," Mr. Foster said as Lauren and Mel ran into the large kitchen. He and Mr. Cassidy were sitting at the table, having coffee.

"We have!" Lauren exclaimed. "We went riding and then Mel showed me around, and she wants to know if I can join her Pony Club." She looked at Mel, who nodded eagerly. "We could go to the meetings together. It would be cool!" Lauren added. "Can I join, Dad?"

Mr. Foster smiled. "It sounds like a great idea."

"I've got the secretary's number somewhere here," Mr. Cassidy said, getting up and rummaging through a pile of papers by the telephone. "Yes, here we are." He wrote it down on a piece of paper and handed it to Mr. Foster. "It's a good Pony Club. The kids learn a lot there. There's a mounted meeting next weekend. Lauren and Twilight are very welcome to have a ride there in our trailer."

"Thanks," said Mr. Foster, taking the paper from him. "I'll call the secretary when we get home."

Lauren and Mel exchanged delighted looks.

"I'm so glad you've moved here," Mel said as Lauren got back on Twilight to ride home.

"Me, too," Lauren said, grinning at her.

"Come on, then," Mr. Foster said, patting Twilight's neck. "Let's go."

Mel ran along the driveway with them. "I'll see you at school tomorrow, Lauren," she called.

"So, do you like Mel?" Mr. Foster said to Lauren as they walked along the road.

"Yeah!" Lauren said. "She's lots of fun." She stroked Twilight's neck. She couldn't stop thinking about Shadow's jumping problem. She really wanted to be able to help. But how?

Maybe Twilight will know, she thought.

CHAPTER

Three

After dinner, Lauren pulled on her sneakers. The sun had just set and she was anxious to get moving. "I'm just going to check on Twilight," she said to her mom.

"OK, honey," Mrs. Foster said. "But don't stay out for too long. Remember, you're starting school tomorrow."

Buddy ran to the door and stood there, his head cocked to one side.

"You're not coming with me, Buddy," Lauren told him. She went outside, shutting the door carefully behind her, and hurried down the path to the paddock. Would Twilight be able to think of a way to help Shadow?

Twilight whickered when he saw her. Lauren began to say the words of the Turning Spell:

Twilight Star, Twilight Star . . .

Suddenly, Twilight whinnied loudly. Lauren stopped. He seemed to be staring at something over her shoulder. She swung around to see what it was.

Buddy was standing on the path behind her.

"Buddy! Go away!" Lauren exclaimed. Buddy was curious enough about Twilight already. If he saw Twilight change into a unicorn, he would never leave him alone. She grabbed hold of the puppy's collar.

"Buddy!" she heard her dad shouting.

"He's here, Dad!" Lauren called back.

Mr. Foster came down the path. "I only opened the door for a second. Buddy just raced off after you. Come on, fella," he said, taking hold of the puppy's collar. "You come in with me."

Lauren waited until she heard the door

of the house shut and then she whispered the secret words.

There was a purple flash and suddenly Twilight was standing before her, a snow-white unicorn once again.

"That was close," he said.

"I know," Lauren said, feeling worried. "I'm going to have to be so careful. Buddy's far too interested in you." Suddenly, she remembered what she'd been going to ask Twilight. "Do you know why Shadow won't jump? Mel's really upset about it."

"I don't know," Twilight admitted. He pawed the grass. "But we could visit him and find out."

"Now?" Lauren said, looking at the sky.

It still wasn't completely dark yet. "But what if Mel or her parents see us?"

"We could go later, then," Twilight said.

Lauren hesitated. "Well, I guess I could come out just after I go to bed," she said. "Mom's writing a new book so she'll be working on her computer, and Dad's bound to be watching TV. But I won't be able to stay out long."

"We'll be quick," Twilight promised.

"All right, then," Lauren agreed. "I'll come back as soon as I can." She said the Undoing Spell, turning Twilight back into a pony, and hurried back to the house.

After her mom had said good night and gone into her study to work, Lauren

pulled her jeans on over her pajamas and
scribbled a quick note for her parents just
in case they came to check on her and
got worried.

I'll be back soon. I've just gone to
see Twilight.
    Lots of love, Lauren XXX

Leaving it on her bed, she crept down the
stairs and out of the house.

I'll be back as quickly as I can, she told
herself as she hurried down to the paddock.

It only took a few seconds to change
Twilight into a unicorn. "Quick!"
Lauren said. She scrambled onto his
back. "Let's go!"

They swooped down on Shadow's
paddock at Goose Creek Farm. "There he
is!" Lauren said, spotting the dark shape
of Mel's dapple-gray pony.

Twilight landed with a soft whicker
just behind him.
Shadow swung
around with
an alarmed
snort.

Twilight whinnied and Lauren saw Shadow relax. He whinnied back as if he was talking to Twilight.

"What's he saying?" Lauren asked Twilight.

"That he knew I was a unicorn," Twilight said. "And he would like to know why we've come."

Lauren didn't want to waste any time. "Ask him why he won't jump," she said to Twilight.

"He understands you," Twilight told her as Shadow whinnied in reply.

Twilight listened to the dapple-gray pony for a few moments. "He's scared," he told Lauren. "He says that when he was a foal, he was jumping over a tree trunk with the other foals in his field and he banged his legs really hard. Ever since then, he's been afraid of jumping. He hates making Mel upset but he just can't do it."

"Have you got any magical powers that could help him not to feel so scared, Twilight?" Lauren asked.

"I don't know," Twilight replied doubtfully. "I know I've got some magical powers, but I'm not sure what they are. I guess I might be able to help, but I don't know how."

Lauren felt disappointed. She'd been hoping that Twilight would be able to do some magic and make everything OK. She thought hard. If they couldn't use Twilight's powers to help Shadow, then maybe she could come up with a more practical solution. "If I put the poles from the jumps on the ground, do you think you might be able to walk over them?" she asked Shadow.

Shadow snorted.

"He says he might," Twilight translated.

"Well, that would be a start," Lauren said. She got off Twilight's back and took two poles and laid them out on the grass. *It's lucky that Shadow's paddock is hidden from the farmhouse,* she thought.

"Try walking over these," she said to Shadow. "At least it's a step toward jumping."

Shadow looked very nervous.

"It'll be OK," Twilight encouraged him.

Shadow walked up to the first pole and stopped. Then, snorting loudly, he stepped over it, picking his hooves up high.

"Well done!" Lauren cried. "Now try the other one, Shadow."

The same thing happened.

"You did it!" Twilight exclaimed as

Shadow trotted back to them, suddenly
looking much happier.

"I'll put up a tiny jump now," Lauren
said. "Let's see if you can do that!"

But Shadow backed off, whinnying.

Twilight sighed. "He doesn't want to. He's still too frightened to try a jump." Shadow neighed. "If we can come and help him some more, he might get braver."

It was better than nothing. "OK, we'll come again tomorrow," Lauren said. She gave Shadow a hug and then got back onto Twilight. "We'll help you, Shadow. No matter how long it takes."

CHAPTER

Four

"Come, on, Lauren!" Mrs. Foster called the next morning.

Lauren checked her reflection for the last time in her bedroom mirror. She was wearing new jeans and a blue T-shirt. Her freshly washed hair was tied back in a ponytail. She swallowed nervously. Her first day at a new school. What was it going to be like?

Taking a deep breath, she ran downstairs. Her mom and Max were waiting by the door.

"Feeling nervous?" Mrs. Foster asked her.

"A little," Lauren admitted, yawning.

Her mom frowned. "Didn't you sleep well last night?"

"I'm fine, Mom," Lauren said quickly. She'd gotten back into the house safely after her adventure with Twilight, and she didn't want her mom getting suspicious now. She picked up her schoolbag. "Come on. Let's go."

Silver River Elementary School was only a ten-minute drive from Granger's Farm. It was a low brick building. As Mrs. Foster parked the car, Lauren saw Mel standing at the school gates. "There's Mel!" she exclaimed.

She jumped out of the car and ran over. "Hi!"

"Hi!" Mel said. "I thought I'd wait for you."

Mrs. Foster and Max walked up to them. "This is my mom and my brother, Max," Lauren said.

"Pleased to meet you," Mel said politely. "I'm in the same class as Lauren, Mrs. Foster. I can show her there if you want."

Mrs. Foster looked questioningly at Lauren, who nodded. "Yeah, I'll be fine, Mom," she said quickly.

"Well, in that case," Mrs. Foster said,

"that would be a real help, Mel. It gives me more time to get Max settled into his classroom. I'll stop by the office, Lauren, and tell them you're here."

"Bye, Mom," said Lauren, giving her a quick kiss. "I'll see you this afternoon."

Mrs. Foster nodded. "I'll pick you up here at the gates. Have a good day, honey."

"She will," Mel said, swinging her schoolbag onto her shoulder. "Come on, Lauren. I want to show you around."

By morning recess, Lauren's nerves had totally disappeared. Mr. Noland, her new teacher, was strict but fun. Even better, he let her and Mel sit together. The other kids in the class seemed really eager to be

friends, too — all except Jade Roberts
and her friend Monica Corder. They
hadn't said a word to Lauren or Mel,
although they had giggled when Jade had
leaned over Mel's desk and caught sight
of a horse that Mel had drawn.

"Looks more like a pig than a horse,"
Jade had said to Monica.

"Or a mule," Monica had said, flicking
her blond hair back.

"Just like her dumb pony," Jade went on,
her green eyes looking mockingly at Mel.
"I mean, imagine having a dumb pony
that won't jump. How sad can you get?"

"He's not dumb!" Lauren said angrily.

Jade turned her full attention to her.
"And what do *you* know about ponies?"

"Well, I've got one," Lauren said.

"Lauren Foster?" Jade said suddenly.
"You're the girl who owns Twilight,
aren't you?" When Lauren nodded,
Jade laughed. "How sad. I got my
dad to sell him because he wasn't
good enough to win ribbons. My
new pony, Prince, is a hundred times
better."

Lauren glared at them but, before she
could say anything, Mr. Noland heard the
whispering and told Jade and Monica to
be quiet.

Lauren was still fuming when the
lesson came to an end.

"Come on, Lauren!" Mel said as they
went outside. "Let's go and sit under the

tree. I've brought some pictures of
Shadow to show you."

"You know, I had an idea last night,"
Lauren said quickly, wanting to cheer her
up. "I think Shadow might be scared
of jumping . . . for some reason. We
could try walking him over poles on
the ground, then, as he gets braver, we
could put up some tiny jumps."

Mel looked doubtful. "Do you really
think it will work?"

"I'm sure," Lauren said. "Look, why
don't I come over after school with
Twilight and we can try then?"

Her enthusiasm seemed to encourage
Mel.

"OK," she said. "Let's do it."

CHAPTER

Five

"Should I try now?" Mel said to Lauren later that afternoon. She was mounted on Shadow and nervously looking at the poles that she and Lauren had laid out on the grass.

"Yes," Lauren said, patting Twilight. "Just trot him over them."

Mel turned Shadow toward the poles. The little dapple-gray pony glanced once at Twilight, then trotted bravely over them.

"He did it!" Mel exclaimed in astonishment.

"I told you!" Lauren said. "Now try again."

So Mel did. By the time Shadow had trotted and cantered over the poles ten times, Mel was beaming from ear to ear. "Maybe I'll be able to get him to jump in the end," she said. She got off Shadow and hugged him. "You're such a good boy!"

Shadow snorted, and Lauren was sure that he looked pleased.

After untacking the ponies and turning them out into Shadow's paddock to graze,

Lauren and Mel went up the path to see Sparkle and her two kittens in the barn.

Star and Midnight were awake. They were toddling around the nest of hay, their heads looking almost too large for their fluffy black bodies.

"Which one's which?" Lauren asked. They looked identical to her.

"Star's got a white star shape on her tummy," Mel explained. She picked up the kitten nearest her. "Look."

"Oh, yes!" Lauren laughed, seeing the white hairs.

"Do you want to hold her?" Mel asked.

Lauren nodded, and Mel handed Star over. The little kitten looked into Lauren's face and then meowed, her mouth opening

so wide that Lauren could see all the way
to the back of her pink throat. "Hello,"
Lauren murmured. "Aren't you cute?"
Star cuddled into her arms.

"Wasn't Shadow good today?" Mel
said to Lauren as she picked up Midnight.

"Yes, he was," Lauren said. "I'm sure he'll learn to jump in the end."

"I hope so," said Mel. "I just wish he could learn in time for the meeting on Saturday. Jade and Monica are being so mean about him, and the only thing that's going to stop them is if he learns to jump." She looked at Lauren hopefully. "Do you think we might get him to jump soon?"

"We might," Lauren said. "Fingers crossed."

As Lauren rode Twilight home, she couldn't stop thinking about Mel's words. Shadow might be able to learn to jump with help, but how long would that take?

It might take ages, and Mel would just continue to get teased.

If only we could teach him to jump more quickly, Lauren thought.

She remembered what Twilight had said about his powers — he had some but he didn't know what they were. Maybe he did have some magic that could help. But how could they find out?

And then the answer came to her. *Mrs. Fontana.* Mrs. Fontana was the only other person in the world who knew Twilight's secret. She'd told Lauren that unicorns existed and had given Lauren an old book that contained the words of the Turning Spell. If anyone would be able to help, she would.

★ ★ ★

As soon as she got home, Lauren ran into the house. Her mom was working on her computer.

"Mom," Lauren said, "can you take me to Mrs. Fontana's bookstore?"

Mrs. Foster frowned. "Why?"

Lauren didn't know what to say. "I . . . I want to ask Mrs. Fontana something," she said. "It's for a project I'm doing. I thought Mrs. Fontana might be able to help."

"Well, actually, I was going to go into town," Mrs. Foster said. "I need to get some film for the camera. Max wants to take some pictures of Buddy to show his teacher. You could go see Mrs. Fontana while I pick up the film."

"Great!" Lauren said.

"Get changed, then," Mrs. Foster said. "We'll go right now."

Almost before Mrs. Foster had parked, Lauren scrambled out of the car.

"I'll meet you there," Mrs. Foster said. "Don't go anywhere else."

"Don't worry, I won't," Lauren promised.

She raced over to the bookstore with its brown-and-gold sign. A chime jangled as she pushed open the door. There was the familiar rose-patterned carpet on the floor, and the air smelled faintly of blackberries. Books spilled off every shelf and surface.

Walter, Mrs. Fontana's terrier, came trotting over as soon as Lauren walked inside. "Hi, boy," Lauren said, bending down to pet him. As she straightened up, she saw that the bookstore owner had appeared, as if by magic. Mrs. Fontana's face was lined and wrinkled, but her blue eyes shone out, bright and clear. She had a mustard-yellow shawl clasped loosely around her shoulders, and her long gray hair was pinned up in a bun.

"Hello, Lauren," she said. "What can I do for you today?"

Lauren hesitated. It was so hard to launch straight into a discussion about unicorns in broad daylight. "Well . . . er . . ."

Mrs. Fontana looked over her shoulder
to where a couple of people were
browsing along a bookshelf. "Come
down to the children's section," she said
softly. "Walter will tell me if I'm needed."

The black-and-white terrier jumped
up onto the counter by the cash register
and sat down, his ears pricked. It was as if
he'd understood every word Mrs. Fontana
had said.

Lauren followed Mrs. Fontana to the
children's section at one side of the shop.
There was an armchair and cushions on
the floor. "So how's Twilight?" Mrs.
Fontana said, sitting down.

"Fine," Lauren replied. She lowered
her voice. "We're trying to help this pony,

Mrs. Fontana. He belongs to my friend, and he's scared of jumping." She quickly explained about Shadow. "He's so scared that it might take ages to get him really jumping," she said. "Do you know if Twilight has any magical powers that could help?"

Mrs. Fontana smiled. "Twilight has many magical powers, Lauren. But I cannot tell you what they are. A unicorn has to discover his powers for himself." She leaned forward and took Lauren's hands in hers. "Don't worry, Twilight *is* able to help this pony," she said. "But it is up to you to help him work out how, Lauren. You became a Unicorn Friend because you have a good heart and the imagination to believe in magic. Use those qualities, and together you and Twilight will discover his powers."

Letting go of Lauren's hands, she straightened up. Her face looked less serious now. "So," she said, her eyes crinkling up at the corners in a smile, "has Buddy found out Twilight's secret yet?"

Lauren stared at her. How had Mrs. Fontana known about the problems she was having with Buddy?

Mrs. Fontana seemed to sense her astonishment. "When I was a Unicorn Friend, I had a dog who was very curious about my unicorn," she explained. "He almost found out my secret several times."

"You had your own unicorn?" Lauren gasped. She'd known that Mrs. Fontana had seen a unicorn, but the woman had never told her that she, too, had once been a Unicorn Friend.

"I did," Mrs. Fontana said softly. "A long time ago."

A hundred questions bubbled up inside Lauren. What had Mrs. Fontana's unicorn been like? What had it been named? How had Mrs. Fontana discovered that it was a unicorn? And, most of all, what had happened to it? Why didn't Mrs. Fontana have it anymore?

But before she could ask any of these questions, Walter barked.

"A customer must need help," Mrs. Fontana said, getting to her feet. She smiled at Lauren. "Good luck with Shadow, Lauren. I hope you and Twilight can find a way to help, and be careful with Buddy. Try not to let him find out Twilight's secret."

With that, Mrs. Fontana went to the front of the shop where someone was waiting to pay for a few books.

The shop door opened, and Mrs. Foster walked in. Lauren ran over. "Hi, Mom."

"Are you ready to go?" Mrs. Foster asked.

Lauren nodded. "Bye, Mrs. Fontana," she said, glancing over to the counter where the bookstore owner was wrapping up the customer's purchases.

Mrs. Fontana looked up. "Good–bye, Lauren," she said. She smiled. "And good luck."

CHAPTER

Six

That evening, Lauren crept out of the house again.

"Are we going to see Shadow?" Twilight asked.

"Yes. Let's be quick," Lauren said, getting onto his back.

As they flew to Goose Creek Farm, she told him what Mrs. Fontana had said. "You have powers that can help," she told him.

"But how can I use them if I don't know what they are?" Twilight said.

"I don't know," Lauren admitted. She'd been thinking the same thing ever since she'd left Mrs. Fontana's shop.

Shadow was waiting for them. He whinnied.

"You were great today, Shadow!" Twilight said as he landed.

Shadow bowed his head, as if a little embarrassed by the praise. He snorted.

"He wants to know if he should try trotting over the poles again," Twilight told Lauren.

"What about trying a small jump?" Lauren suggested hopefully.

Shadow looked worried.

"Go on, just try," Twilight said.

Shadow hesitated for a moment and then slowly nodded.

Before Shadow could change his mind, Lauren scrambled off Twilight and put up a tiny jump. "You can do it, Shadow!" she said.

Shadow nodded and, turning toward the jump, he began to trot.

"He's going to do it!" Lauren gasped to Twilight.

But then Shadow stopped dead.

"Oh, no." Lauren sighed.

She and Twilight trotted over. Shadow was standing a few feet away from the jump. "What's wrong?" Lauren asked him. "Why did you stop?"

The dapple-gray pony hung his head and snorted sadly.

"He was just too scared," Twilight told Lauren.

Shadow looked so dejected that Lauren was sure that if ponies could cry, he would have been in tears.

Twilight stepped forward and touched his glowing horn to Shadow's neck. "It's OK," Lauren heard him say softly. "You tried your best. Don't be upset."

They stood there for a moment, and then Lauren saw the little dapple-gray pony's ears flicker forward. He raised his head and whickered in a surprised sort of way.

"What's he saying?" Lauren asked Twilight.

"That he's feeling a little better,"
Twilight replied.

Shadow whickered again.

"Much better," Twilight said.

Lauren saw Shadow look at the jump.
His eyes suddenly seemed to be full of
confidence. He whinnied.

"In fact, he says he feels so much
better that he thinks he might be able to
clear the jump," Twilight said, looking
astonished.

Shadow pricked up his ears and trotted
away from them. Turning toward the
jump, he started to canter. Lauren and
Twilight watched in amazement as he
flew over it.

"He jumped it!" Lauren exclaimed.

Shadow came cantering back to them, whinnying.

"He says that when we were talking he suddenly felt really brave," Twilight said, stamping his front hoof in excitement. "He says he's never felt like that before, but it was as if he just knew he could do it."

Shadow nuzzled Twilight and suddenly Lauren's eyes widened. "Your horn!" she exclaimed to Twilight. "You were touching him with your horn when he started to feel brave. Maybe that's one of your magical powers. Maybe by touching him you gave him your courage — a unicorn's bravery."

Shadow tossed his head and whinnied.

"He says he doesn't care what hap-pened, he's just glad that he could do it," Twilight said.

Shadow nodded, and then he turned and cantered over the jump again.

Lauren hugged Twilight in delight. "This is fantastic!" she said. "Mel is going to be so pleased." Her heart sang. She couldn't wait to see her friend's face when she jumped with Shadow tomorrow!

Lauren was even more pleased by their night's work when Jade started teasing Mel again the next day at lunchtime.

"Still planning on going to the meeting on Saturday, Mel?" Jade asked, coming over to them as they put their trays away. "I don't know why you're bothering. It's not like Shadow will jump. Can't your parents afford to buy you a better pony?"

"Mel doesn't want another pony," Lauren said, unable to bear their teasing a second longer. "Shadow's fine."

Jade laughed. "Yeah, right," she said,
walking off laughing.

Lauren looked at her friend. Mel was
biting her lip in frustration. "She's so mean!"
she burst out. "I think I'm just going to tell
Dad that I don't want to go on Saturday."

"You can't," Lauren said. "You've got to come, Mel. If you don't, Jade and Monica will tease you again next week." Mel looked even more miserable. "Shadow will be good," Lauren went on. "In fact, when you ride him today I'm sure he's going to jump."

Mel looked at her doubtfully. "You think so?"

"I know so," Lauren said confidently.

As soon as Lauren got home after school, she gave Twilight a quick brush over and rode him to Mel's. "I can't wait to see her face when Shadow jumps," Lauren said to him as they trotted along the road.

Mel was just putting Shadow's saddle

on when they arrived. When they rode into the paddock, Lauren set up the jump exactly as she had done the night before. Then she got back on Twilight. "Try Shadow now!" she called to Mel.

"OK," Mel said. She turned Shadow toward the jump. His ears pricked up, and he quickened his stride.

"He's going to jump it!" Lauren whispered to Twilight in delight.

Shadow got nearer and nearer, his hooves thudding on the grass.

Then, a yard in front of the jump, he suddenly stopped.

CHAPTER

Seven

Lauren gasped in disappointment. After last night, she'd been sure that Shadow was going to jump.

Twilight snorted, and Lauren knew he was just as surprised as she was that Shadow had stopped.

Mel turned the dapple-gray pony away from the jump. "I'll try him again," she called. "It almost felt like he was going to jump it then." But when she tried again, Shadow wouldn't go anywhere near the jump.

Mel rode back to Lauren looking bitterly disappointed. "I guess I should have known better than to think he would jump it," she said. Shadow hung his head sadly. Mel hugged him. "Don't worry, boy. I still love you."

Despite her words, Shadow looked very upset. He didn't prick his ears up once, not even when they played catch.

"I think I'll take him in," Mel said at last. "He doesn't seem very happy."

Lauren nodded. "I'm sorry, Mel," she said as they dismounted.

"It's not your fault," Mel said with a sigh.

Lauren didn't hang around for long. She had a feeling that Mel wanted to be on her own and so, after a while, she got back on Twilight and rode him home.

"What went wrong?" she said to him. "Why didn't Shadow jump?"

Twilight shook his head and snorted.

"I'll come down to your paddock tonight," Lauren told him. "We've got to figure this out."

She was grooming Twilight back at Granger's Farm when Buddy came running down the path toward them. He skidded to a stop and began to sniff around Twilight's hooves.

"Buddy, go away!" Lauren said.

Buddy sat down and, cocking his head to one side, whined at Twilight.

Just then, Max came running down the path. "There you are, Buddy!" he said as the puppy trotted over to meet him. Buddy licked his hand and then turned back to Twilight and woofed.

Max frowned. "Why does Buddy act so weird around Twilight, Lauren?"

"I don't know," Lauren said. "Look, I'm trying to groom him. Why don't you take Buddy for a walk, Max?"

But Max didn't seem to be listening. Suddenly, his eyes widened as he looked at Twilight. "Maybe Twilight's an alien, Lauren!" He gasped.

"An alien!" Lauren stared at him.

"Yeah, maybe Twilight's an alien from another planet. He's in disguise so that he can spy on us, and Buddy knows it!"

"Don't be silly, Max. Twilight's just a

pony," Lauren said, desperately trying to act as if Max were totally crazy.

"So why does Buddy act so weird around him, then?" Max said.

"Because . . . because he's not used to ponies," Lauren said quickly.

But Max didn't look convinced. "I'm going to tell Mom," he said and, turning, he ran back up the path.

Lauren stared after him. She was sure her mom would just laugh at Max's idea about aliens, but the last thing she wanted was Max going on and on saying that there was something odd about Twilight.

"You see all the trouble you're causing?" she said to Buddy, who was sniffing at Twilight's tail.

CHAPTER

Eight

It was Lauren's turn to help wash the dishes after supper. Once they were all dried and put away, she pulled on her boots. "I'm going to see Twilight, Mom," she said.

"OK," Mrs. Foster said. She looked around. "Has anyone seen Max?"

Lauren and her dad shook their heads.

Mrs. Foster smiled. "He's probably in his room drawing aliens."

"Or Twilight's spaceship," Mr. Foster said with a laugh.

Lauren let herself out the back door, feeling very relieved that her mom and dad were treating her brother's suspicions as a joke.

"Hi, boy," she called as Twilight whinnied to her from the paddock gate. "Do you know why Shadow wouldn't jump today?" she asked Twilight as soon as she had turned him into a unicorn.

"No," Twilight replied.

"Let's go see him," Lauren said. "There has to be a reason."

Twilight flew to Shadow's field. The little dapple-gray pony was standing quietly, still looking very unhappy.

"Oh, Shadow," Lauren said, sliding off Twilight's back and going over to him. "What went wrong today? Why couldn't you jump?"

Shadow whinnied.

"Oh," Twilight said. He turned to

Lauren. "Poor Shadow. He says he really wanted to, but he just didn't feel brave enough without the touch of my horn."

Shadow neighed sadly.

Lauren didn't like to see Shadow looking so upset. "I don't know what to do," she told Shadow. "You know Twilight can't be a unicorn when there are other people around."

Shadow nodded.

He didn't try jumping again that evening. After all, they knew he *could* jump at night when Twilight was a unicorn—it was jumping in the day that was the problem.

Lauren sighed unhappily as she and

Twilight flew home. She really wished there was something they could do to help.

The next morning at school, Mel looked serious. "I've decided that I'm not going to try to jump Shadow ever again," she told Lauren. "It just makes him so miserable and I'd rather get teased than make him unhappy."

"What will you do about the meeting on Saturday?" Lauren asked.

"I'll have to say that I don't want to jump him." Mel glanced across the classroom to where Jade and Monica were sitting. "And I'll just have to put up with whatever those two say."

Lauren squeezed her arm comfortingly. "Ignore them."

"Easier said than done." Mel sighed. She forced a smile on her face. "Will you still come over with Twilight this afternoon, though? We could go for a trail ride."

Lauren nodded. "Sure," she said.

When Lauren got to Goose Creek Farm that afternoon, Mel was already mounted on Shadow. "We'd better get going," Mel said. "Mom thinks there might be a storm coming."

Lauren looked up at the overcast sky. The air certainly had a heavy, stormy feel about it.

They rode up the path toward the woods. Mr. Cassidy was fixing a fence near the hay barn. "Don't go out too far," he called.

"We'll stay close to the farm," Mel promised. "Come on, Lauren! Let's go."

They urged Shadow and Twilight into a trot.

"Let's go into the woods," Mel said. "There's a great trail there with a sandy part where we can have a canter."

"OK," Lauren said, shortening Twilight's reins. His ears flickered back and forth. "Come on, boy," she said encouragingly.

A few minutes later, they entered the woods. The tops of the tall trees met over their heads like a green ceiling. Lauren smiled to herself. What would Mel say if she knew that Twilight had jumped over those very treetops with Lauren on his back?

"Here's the long canter," Mel said. The trail stretched out in front of them, straight and inviting. "Are you ready?"

Lauren nodded.

Mel leaned forward and gave Shadow his head. The dapple-gray pony bounded into a canter. Twilight hesitated for a moment and then, when Lauren squeezed his side, he followed.

The wind whipped against Lauren's face as she leaned forward and urged Twilight on. His hooves thudded down on the sand, and she could feel a broad grin stretch across her face. This was as good as flying!

At last, the trail began to narrow and they slowed Twilight and Shadow to a trot and then to a walk. Both ponies we're breathing hard from the canter, so Lauren and Mel let them walk for a while.

Suddenly, they heard a deep, low, rumbling noise. The leaves on the branches nearest to them seemed to shiver slightly.

"Thunder!" Mel said, looking at Lauren in alarm. "We'd better turn around."

As they began to trot back along the

trail, they heard a pitter-pattering of rain on the leafy canopy above them.

Mel nodded and Shadow and Twilight began to canter along the path. Lauren felt worried. Her parents had warned her lots of times about not being out in a thunderstorm.

As they reached the entrance to the woods, Lauren reined Twilight in. A jagged flash of lightning forked down, lighting up the darkened sky.

"M-maybe we should stay here," Mel stammered, looking frightened.

"No, it's really dangerous to stay near trees," Lauren said. "The lightning might strike one of them." She looked down the path toward the house. "If we gallop, we'll be back in a minute," she said, looking at the lights shining invitingly out of the farmhouse's windows. "Come on!"

She leaned forward, and Twilight plunged out from the trees.

"Come on, Twilight," Lauren urged, leaning low over his neck like a jockey. Twilight's hooves pounded as he galloped down the track, passing the hay barn and heading toward the barn with Shadow's stall.

Suddenly, Lauren saw Mel's dad standing in the barn's entrance.

Reaching Mr. Cassidy, Twilight skidded to a halt. Shadow was only a few feet behind.

"Quick!" Mr. Cassidy shouted above

the noise of the storm. "Get into the barn before the rain gets any heavier!"

Lauren and Mel flung themselves off Twilight's and Shadow's backs and ran with them inside.

"I've never seen a storm blow up so quickly," Mr. Cassidy said.

Suddenly, there was a clap of thunder and, at the same time, the sky outside lit up with a bright white flash of lightning. There was a loud bang nearby.

Mr. Cassidy ran to the entrance and looked out. "A tree by the hay barn's been hit. It's on fire!" he exclaimed. "I'm going to have to call the fire department. You stay here while I go to the house. I don't want you outside in this."

"But what about the fire?" Mel cried.

"It's all right. It won't reach you here," Mr. Cassidy said. "I'll be back as soon as I can." And with that, he ducked his head and ran out.

Lauren led Twilight to the entrance and looked up the trail toward the hay barn. The tall oak tree that stood next to it was burning brightly.

Mel joined her. "If it falls, the whole barn will go up in flames! Dad had better be —" She broke off, her eyes widening. "Sparkle!" she cried in horror. "Lauren! Sparkle and her kittens are inside!"

CHAPTER

Nine

Mel put her foot in the stirrup and swung herself up onto Shadow's back.

"What are you doing?" Lauren exclaimed.

"I've got to save Sparkle," Mel said, digging her heels into Shadow's sides and heading out.

"It's too dangerous, Mel!" Lauren cried.

But it was too late. Mel was already cantering Shadow up the trail toward the barn.

Lauren didn't hesitate. Swinging herself up on Twilight's back, she galloped after her friend. "Mel! Stop!" she yelled. She hated the thought of Sparkle and the kittens being trapped in the barn, but she knew Mel's life could be in danger if she went inside.

But Mel didn't listen. She urged Shadow past the burning tree and up to the barn door. Jumping off his back, she hauled it open.

Sparkle came racing out. She was carrying one of the kittens in her mouth. Lauren saw a flash of white on the kitten's tummy. Star! But what about Midnight? He must still be inside.

To her horror, Lauren saw Mel loop Shadow's reins over her arm and run into the barn.

Twilight gave an alarmed whinny. There was a loud creak. Lauren looked up. A huge burning branch of the oak tree looked as if it was about to break off.

"Mel!" she shouted. "Get out!"

Mel appeared on foot in the doorway of the barn, clutching Midnight.

"Quick!" Lauren yelled, looking up at the tree.

But it was too late. Before Mel could get out of the barn, there was a loud

crack and the burning branch crashed to
the ground in front of the barn door.

Mel screamed and Lauren gasped. The
branch was blocking the way out!

Lauren could see Mel's terrified eyes through the smoke that was filling the air. There was only one way for her to get out.

"Get up on Shadow and make him jump the branch, Mel!" Lauren cried. "It's the only way."

"But he won't do it!" Mel shouted.

"Just try!" Lauren called.

Clutching Midnight to her chest, Mel scrambled onto Shadow's back.

Lauren glanced around, desperately hoping to see Mr. Cassidy or the fire department arriving, but there was no one there. "Shadow, please!" she yelled as Mel began to trot him toward the log. "You've got to jump it! For Mel!"

She heard Shadow neigh uncertainly

through the smoke. *Please jump it,* Lauren
prayed. *You might not have Twilight's magical
powers to help you, but you can still do it.
Please, Shadow, please!*

She saw Shadow hesitate and dread
gripped her heart. He wasn't going to be
able to do it.

"Melanie!" Hearing a hoarse cry,
Lauren swung around. Mr. Cassidy was
running up the hill toward them, looking
horrified. For a moment, Lauren felt
a surge of hope but then her heart
plummeted. It was obvious that Mr.
Cassidy couldn't move the log on his
own. There was still only one way for
Mel to get out and that was for Shadow
to jump.

Twilight seemed to realize the same thing. Throwing his head back, he whinnied loudly to Shadow. As he did so, a fork of lightning flashed across the sky, making every hair of his gray body shine with a bright white light.

Suddenly, Lauren saw a new look of bravery flash into Shadow's eyes. Tossing his head back just like Twilight, he broke into a canter. Mel grabbed hold of his mane with her free hand. Shadow's stride lengthened. His ears pricked and the next second, he was soaring over the burning log, clearing it with ease.

Mel was hanging on to Midnight, a look of astonishment, relief, and delight on her face as they galloped up to

Twilight. "He did it!" she said, sliding off
Shadow's back as he halted. "He jumped
it, Lauren! He actually jumped it."

"He was amazing!" Lauren cried, and Twilight whinnied in agreement.

Just then, Mr. Cassidy reached them. "Mel! Oh, my goodness," he said, his breath coming in short gasps. "I thought you weren't going to get out. What were you doing in the hay barn?"

"R-rescuing Midnight," Mel stammered.

"But I told you not to leave the barn," Mr. Cassidy said, pulling her into his arms and kissing her. "I'm just so glad you're safe."

"And it's all because of Shadow," Mel said, breaking free and hugging the dapple-gray pony. "Isn't he wonderful, Dad?"

Mr. Cassidy smiled at Shadow. "The best."

Shadow whickered proudly, happiness lighting up his dark eyes.

As the fire crew arrived and began to put out the fire, Mr. Cassidy helped the girls make up a special feed of warm bran, carrots, and molasses for Shadow and Twilight. Once the two ponies were dry and settled down in the two stalls, Lauren and Mel went inside.

"I can hardly move I feel so tired," Mel said as she and Lauren kicked off their boots by the back door.

"Me, too," Lauren agreed.

Mrs. Cassidy was waiting for them.

She was upset with Mel for taking such a risk but she was so relieved that both girls were safe that she made them enormous mugs of hot chocolate with marshmallows floating on top.

As Lauren looked out of the kitchen to where the fire crew was saying good-bye to Mr. Cassidy, she breathed a sigh of relief. Luckily, the flames hadn't spread to the hay barn, so Mr. Cassidy's hay was OK.

In fact, Lauren thought, *everything turned out OK*. She and Mel and both horses were safe. Midnight the kitten had been reunited with Sparkle, and Mel had made the little family a new bed in the stall next to Shadow.

Lauren shivered as she realized that it could have all been so different. If it hadn't been for Shadow's bravery, she didn't like to think of what might have happened. She remembered the way he had hesitated as he'd approached the log. How had he suddenly found the courage that he needed to jump it?

That night, when Lauren turned Twilight into a unicorn, she asked him if he knew how Shadow had found the courage to jump.

"No, I don't," Twilight admitted. "Shall we go visit him to find out?"

Lauren mounted and, with a kick of

Twilight's back legs, they rose into the night sky.

Shadow was grazing near the bottom of his moonlit paddock. Lauren jumped off Twilight's back and ran over to him. "You were amazing today, Shadow," she said as he whinnied a greeting. "I didn't think you were going to do it but you were so brave. What made you able to jump?"

Shadow neighed.

"He says that when the lightning flashed it made me look like a unicorn," Twilight translated for Lauren. "He realized that if he was going to save Mel, he had to be as brave as he was the other night when my horn touched him — as brave as a unicorn."

Lauren nodded, remembering the look that had come into Shadow's eyes as the lightning had shone on Twilight's coat. It all made sense. She looked at the dapple-gray pony. "Well, you were wonderful, Shadow and, best of all, now that you've jumped that great big log, the jumps at the Pony Club will seem tiny. You'll be able to jump them easily."

Shadow snorted doubtfully.

"He doesn't think so," Twilight interpreted. "He says that he could only jump the log because he had to."

Lauren frowned. "But Twilight wasn't a unicorn when you jumped that log,

Shadow. You jumped that log because you were brave."

Twilight whickered in agreement.

Shadow stared at Lauren as if she'd said something totally astonishing.

"You saved Mel's life, Shadow," Lauren said softly. "If you can do that, you can do anything."

A new look of confidence began to shine in Shadow's eyes.

Lauren climbed onto Twilight's back. "We'd better go," she said. "Good night, Shadow."

Shadow whinnied proudly and tossed his mane as Lauren rode Twilight off into the night.

★ ★ ★

On Saturday afternoon, Lauren stood beside Twilight, watching Mel ride Shadow toward the first jump in the course that Kathy, their Pony Club trainer, had set out.

It had taken a lot for Lauren to persuade Mel to try the jumping course but, after being reminded of Shadow's huge leap over the burning log, she had finally agreed.

"I don't know why Mel's bothering." Jade's snide voice cut through the air. She was watching with Monica. "Shadow's never going to make a course of jumps — last month he wouldn't even jump one."

Lauren didn't say anything. She just

crossed her fingers. The course was small but twisty, and no one in the group had managed a clear round yet.

Jade's pony, Prince, had knocked three fences over, and Monica's pony, Scout, had had three refusals. Twilight had only knocked one fence down, which Lauren didn't mind at all because she knew he'd tried his best. She crossed her fingers as Mel cantered Shadow toward the first jump.

She held her breath. Would Shadow stop?

But, to her delight, the dapple-gray pony's ears pricked up, his stride lengthened, and he jumped perfectly over the fence. He cantered to the next one and then the next. As he cleared the last fence, everyone burst into applause for a perfect clear round.

Mel patted Shadow as if she were never going to stop.

Seeing the happiness on Mel's and Shadow's faces, Lauren hugged Twilight in delight. "Oh, Twilight, isn't it great?" she whispered. "I'm so glad you were able to help."

Twilight shook his head and pushed his nose against her chest.

Lauren understood him perfectly. "OK, then," she said, putting her arm around his neck. "I'm so glad *we* were able to help!"